DISC

	DATE DUE		

UNDER THE WATERFALL

SUSANNAH BRIN

ꓵꓵꓵ *Artesian* **Press**
P.O. Box 355 Buena Park, CA 90621

Take Ten Books
Fantasy

Under The Waterfall	**1-58659-064-2**
Cassette	**1-58659-069-3**
The Cooler King	1-58659-061-8
Cassette	1-58659-066-9
Ken and the Samurai	1-58659-062-6
Cassette	1-58659-067-7
The Wishstone	1-58659-065-0
Cassette	1-58659-070-7
The Rabbit Tattoo	1-58659-063-4
Cassette	1-58659-068-5

Other Take Ten Themes:

Mystery
Sports
Adventure
Chillers
Thrillers
Disaster

Project Editor: Dwayne Epstein
Illustrations: Fujiko
Graphic Design: Tony Amaro
©2001 Artesian Press

Artesian **Press**   ISBN 1-58659-064-2

CONTENTS

CHAPTER 1

Matt Pherson watched his older brother push his way through the thick undergrowth of the forest. "Hey, Adam! Don't you think we should turn back? We don't know this part of the forest," Matt yelled.

Up ahead, Adam stopped and looked back at Matt. "I want to find the waterfall. I have a feeling we're close. But, hey, if you're scared, little brother, then go home," Adam grinned.

"I'm not scared," Matt yelled back. He remembered stories of people getting lost in the forest and never being found, not even their bones. He glanced up through the thick branches of the fir trees. The sky was dark with clouds.

Matt unwrapped a piece of gum from his pocket and popped it into his mouth. Immediately, he felt better. He didn't know why, but chewing gum always gave him a shot of confidence. He watched Adam pushing his way through the thick bushes ahead. Adam's red jacket was bright as a berry against the deep green of the forest.

"I wonder if I'll be fearless when I'm seventeen, like Adam?" thought Matt. "Who am I kidding? I'm not going to change in a year. I'll probably always be the brother afraid to take chances." Matt shook his head with disgust. As much as he wanted to be like his brother, he found himself always taking the safe route. Adam rushed at life with total fearlessness.

"Hey, Matt, get moving. We're never going to find the waterfall with you dragging your feet," Adam yelled.

"I'm coming," Matt grumbled. He

stomped on a blackberry vine that threatened to tangle around his boot. Tiny branches grabbed at his clothes and scratched at his face as he pushed his way through dried brush and overgrown plants. The dead twigs broke under his boots with a loud snap.

"This is crazy. Hiking around out here, in the middle of winter, looking for a waterfall that probably doesn't exist," mumbled Matt. "I don't know why I let Adam talk me into coming out here."

But he did know. He couldn't say no to his brother's wild ideas because Adam made everything sound like an exciting adventure.

Suddenly, Adam came running back through the trees. His breath steamed near Matt's face as he jogged in a circle around him. "You are slower than a porcupine crossing the road on a hot day," Adam teased.

"Get out of my face, man," Matt

7

snapped, giving his brother a push.

Adam laughed, a big booming laugh. "Come on, Matt, loosen up. Enjoy the day. It's great out here." Adam took a deep breath like he was inhaling the great outdoors.

"I don't have to get myself lost in the woods to have a great day," grumbled Matt. "Besides, it's cold, and it's going to snow any minute."

Adam laughed again. He slapped Matt on the back. "The cold is good for you. And besides, I know where we are. Old Man Barker gave me a map. It says the falls drop over a thousand feet into a huge pool of blue water."

Matt shook his head. "Old Man Barker is full of it. How come no one else has ever seen this waterfall?"

Adam shrugged, unconcerned. "Maybe no one's ever tried looking for it."

"No, it's because it doesn't exist,"

Matt said. The air seemed to have grown colder in the few minutes they'd stood arguing. "I think we should head for home. We don't want to get caught out here in a snow storm," Matt said.

Adam pulled a hand-drawn map from his pocket and studied it. "I think we're almost there. Another ten or twenty minutes. But hey, if you want to chicken out, go right ahead."

"I'm not chickening out. I just think we should turn back before the snow comes," Matt argued.

"It's not going to snow. But do what you want, little brother," said Adam. He broke into a jog and headed off.

"Hardhead," muttered Matt. He watched Adam plunge through a thicket of bushes. Sighing, he followed after his brother. Seconds later, he felt a drop of something cold hit his face, then another and another. All around him, snow flakes were falling like feathers loosened from a pillow.

"I knew it. We should have turned back," Matt said aloud. "This is crazy. We're going to get caught out here and freeze to death!" He broke into a jog to catch his brother and talk some sense into him. Suddenly, Matt felt his foot get caught under a fallen tree limb. He hit the forest floor hard, knocking the wind from his body.

When he tried to stand, his ankle stung with pain. He sat back down.

"Oh, great. This is just what I need," said Matt angrily. He looked at the ground and saw a weathered gray stick of wood, the size and length of a walking stick. Matt grabbed it and used it to pull himself to a standing position. The stick in his hand felt warm. He glanced at it, and for a split second, thought he saw the face of a bearded man in the wood.

Matt shook his head, thinking his

eyes were playing tricks on him. He looked in the direction he'd last seen Adam. Adam was gone. "Adam!" yelled Matt. Using the stick, he limped forward, shouting his brother's name. Adam didn't answer. The forest was as silent as a tomb.

CHAPTER 2

Using the stick for support, Matt limped on, looking for his brother. He called to him over and over. Adam didn't answer. He searched the damp forest floor for footprints. He looked for anything that might show where Adam had gone. He found nothing. Adam had vanished.

"I've got to get help," thought Matt. He noticed the snow beginning to form a layer of white, frosting the tree branches like icing on a cake. He studied the area, trying to fix the spot in his mind. Everything looked alike. Giant fir trees, spruces and pines towered above him, their branches touching and woven together.

"I've got to leave something to mark this spot," Matt said worrying. Then it came to him. "I'll leave my hat." He flipped off his orange baseball cap and secured it to the lowest tree branch he could find. His ankle throbbed with pain. He didn't care. His only thought was getting home and getting help.

He called out to Adam one last time. Getting no answer, Matt hobbled as fast as he could toward home.

It was night when Matt reached the edge of the forest. Knife-like pain ripped up his leg with every step he took. He was shivering with cold. The only place on his body that was warm was his hand that held the walking stick.

Across the snowy field, he saw lights burning in every window of the house, the horse barn and the outside poles that lit the driveway. "Dad!" Matt yelled. Not getting an answer, Matt forced himself to move faster.

13

When he reached the house, Matt slammed through the back door into the kitchen yelling, "Dad! Dad!"

A tall man with a muscular build and the look of someone used to being in command, strode into the kitchen. With a glance at Matt's snow covered, limping body, his look of surprise turned to worry. "Matt, what's happened? Where's Adam?" Harvey Pherson's strong voice edged with worry. He helped Matt over to one of the chairs circling the kitchen table.

"Adam and I went out in the forest looking for that waterfall Old Man Barker is always talking about," Matt said with tears in his eyes.

"And what happened, Matt?" Mr. Pherson asked impatiently.

"Adam got ahead of me. I tripped and sprained my ankle. When I got up, Adam was gone. I looked for him everywhere, Dad. He just vanished. Then I came back here for help." Matt took another deep breath to keep from crying.

Harvey Pherson squeezed his son's shoulder, then grabbed the phone on the kitchen counter. "You did the right thing," Matt's Dad said as he dialed. "I'll get Sheriff Williams to organize a search party. Now, get out of those wet clothes."

As Matt hobbled down the hall to put on dry clothes, he heard his father curse, then slam down the phone. Matt turned back to the kitchen.

"Phone's out," Matt's Dad said. "A line must have gone down somewhere. I'm going into town to get help." He grabbed a heavy parka from the coat rack in the hall.

"I'll go with you," Matt said.

"No, you get into some dry clothes and sit by the fire until I get back." A faraway look came into Harvey Pherson's eyes. He shook his head as he drew on his parka and said, "If you're mother were still alive, she'd fix that ankle of yours right up."

"I know, Dad. I miss her too," Matt answered. She'd been dead over two years, and he still thought about her every day.

"I'll be back," Harvey Pherson said as he left the house.

Matt changed into dry blue jeans and a heavy sweater. He limped into Adam's room and rummaged around in Adam's dresser. Adam was always hurting himself playing some sport, so Matt knew he'd find an assortment of ace bandages. He wrapped a bandage around his ankle, carefully drew on a pair of wool socks and then some old ski boots. He winced with pain as he tried putting weight on his swollen ankle. Grabbing the walking stick, he hobbled into the living room.

Matt threw a log on the already blazing fire, then sank into an armchair to wait for his father. He dropped the

16

walking stick by the side of the chair. He glanced out at the snow coming down in sheets. He prayed his brother had found a cave to shelter him from the storm.

The heat from the fire made his eyes grow heavy. Exhaustion and the warmth from the fire were too much for Matt. He fell asleep.

Minutes later, Matt was awake. His chair was shaking violently. The table lamps were swaying on the tables. "We're having an earthquake in a snow storm," Matt yelled to the empty house. He then looked at the fireplace.

Pacing in front of the fire, dressed in old leather clothes, was the tallest and biggest man Matt had ever seen.

CHAPTER 3

The stranger, dressed in the leather of an ancient woodsman, was ten feet tall with arms and legs like tree trunks.

"Who are you and where did you come from?" Matt asked. His heart beat like a hammer inside his chest.

"Do not be frightened. I am Odhar. I am from the forest." Odhar's voice was like the roar of a running river.

"How did you get in here?" asked Matt.

Odhar's sky blue eyes twinkled. "You brought me here."

"Me?"

"You leaned on me when you walked home."

"What are you talking about?" Matt asked.

18

"I was your walking stick," Odhar answered. He was chuckling at the surprise he saw on Matt's face.

Matt reached over the side of his chair for the stick. It was gone. "You're the face in the wood I saw?"

"Aye. I've been trapped in the stick for almost a hundred years, waiting for someone to come along and break the spell," Odhar explained.

"What spell? What are you talking about?" Shakily, Matt got to his feet. Nothing was making sense.

"Baron Everil, Master of the Underworld, put a spell on me. He turned me into a stick of wood. When you touched me, you broke the spell."

"I don't understand," Matt said, still cautious of the huge man.

Odhar wrinkled up his nut brown face like he was trying to find a way to explain everything. "I helped you walk. I supported your weight. I did good. Good overcomes evil, and doing good can break any spell. Baron Everil and I have been battling since time began." The wooden floor groaned under his weight as Odhar crossed to the window. Outside, snowflakes as big as cotton balls were falling.

Matt limped across the room to where Odhar stood at the window. Seeing the piling snowdrifts, he suddenly remembered his brother Adam, alone and cold, somewhere in the forest. He glanced at the clock on the fireplace mantel. His father had been gone over an hour. He should have been back by now. He jerked his eyes upward at Odhar. "Do you know where my brother is?"

Odhar nodded. "Baron Everil has taken him. Every hundred years, he takes a human back to his home, below the waterfall."

Matt could hardly breathe. Old Man Barker was right, there was a waterfall in the forest. "What will this evil Baron

The woodsman towered over Matt.

do to my brother?" he whispered.

Odhar hesitated as if he was trying to decide whether to tell Matt the terrible truth. Finally, he said, "Baron

Everil will eat your brother to celebrate the Winter of Darkness that begins at midnight tonight."

Horrified, Matt looked at the clock. It read ten o'clock. "Two hours. We've only got two hours to rescue my brother."

Limping as fast as he could, Matt reached for his pack of gum and the pocket knife he'd taken from his wet clothes earlier. He jammed the gum and pocket knife in his coat pocket and headed for the front door.

As Matt reached for the door handle, he felt Odhar's hand fall onto his shoulder like a ton of bricks, stopping him. "What is it?" he asked, twisting to look up at the giant.

"Rescuing your brother won't be easy. Baron Everil is a very powerful ruler. He has an army of fierce warriors. The last time I saved a human from his grasp, I was wounded. That's when he put the spell on me," explained Odhar. His long shaggy brown hair hung around his face and rustled as he shook his huge head.

"Are you afraid?" Matt asked, knowing he was more frightened.

Odhar laughed a big belly laugh that rattled the windows. Then, he frowned. "No, I am not afraid of anything above or below ground. Baron Everil's warriors can sense fear. If they do, they will be on you faster than wolves on a wounded deer."

Matt swallowed hard. "I don't have a choice in this. I have to save my brother." A blast of cold air hit Matt in the face as he flung open the front door.

CHAPTER 4

The night sky was dark gray with clouds. The cold wind whipped the snow flakes around like dancing dots. Matt had only gone a few feet from the house when he sank into a deep snow drift. He struggled to get up, cursing his sprained ankle. Odhar appeared by his side and easily lifted Matt to his feet.

"Tall as me, fit as me, I make you be," chanted Odhar, clamping his big hand on Matt's shoulder.

Suddenly, Matt grew ten feet tall. His arms and legs broke the seams of his clothes. He took a step forward on his sprained ankle. It no longer hurt. Matt grinned with delight. "Wow, Odhar. How did you do that?"

Odhar shrugged. "Simple magic." He turned and headed across the snowy field. Tall as Odhar now, with his ankle fixed, Matt had no trouble keeping up.

A freezing wind blew stinging snow across the field. "Can you make it stop snowing with some of your magic?" Matt yelled at Odhar.

Odhar shook his snow crusted head. "Wish that I could. Weather has a power all its own. Don't worry. We're almost to the forest."

Matt lifted his head. Odhar was right. The edge of the forest was a few feet away. "We're coming, Adam. Just hang on," Matt thought to himself.

Entering the snow covered forest, Matt was struck by its beauty. The boughs of the evergreen trees were gracefully bent under the weight of the snow. The forest floor was a bumpy carpet of white.

Matt shivered, sensing a sinister

presence moving beneath the snow layer. For a moment, a deadly stillness filled the forest. Then suddenly, the wind came back, moaning soft and low. Fear swept through Matt's body freezing him in his tracks.

"Why have you stopped?" Odhar asked.

Matt frowned and avoided Odhar's piercing stare. He glanced over the area and said, "The snow has covered my tracks. I don't know how to get back to where I last saw Adam. I left my baseball hat as a marker."

"Never mind the hat. Follow me," Odhar snapped. "Hurry yourself. We do not have much time."

Matt nodded. He popped a piece of gum in his mouth. Immediately, he felt some of his confidence return as the tangy-sweet flavors of the gum swished inside his mouth.

As they pressed forward through the knee-high snow, Matt kept an eye out for a sign of something familiar. He saw nothing but snow covered forest before his eyes without a sign of anything, especially not the waterfall.

Matt was about ready to curse Odhar and his wild tale of an evil Baron when suddenly, a great waterfall seemed to come out of the very air before him. It was rising from the snow where before, there had been nothing but fir trees.

Rubbing his eyes, Matt looked again. Water dropped from a high rocky cliff into a pool of the deepest green-blue water he had ever seen. Great chunks of ice hung on the rocks surrounding the waterfall. A powdery snow called rime circled the edge of the pool.

"There's beauty even in evil," Odhar sighed, watching Matt stare at the waterfall. He clapped a hand on Matt's shoulder and squeezed. "Time to go swimming. The entrance to Baron

Odhar and Matt stared at the waterfall.

Everil's world is 200 feet down."

"I can't hold my breath that long," protested Matt. He stared at the pool of water. If he didn't run out of breath, he knew he would freeze to death.

"Fear is your constant companion, isn't it, boy? You're just going to have to believe you can do this, and you can," Odhar said.

At the edge of the pool, Matt hesitated. He thought about how his life would be without his brother. Glancing at Odhar, he took a deep breath to steady himself. "Okay, I'm ready."

"Swim like the salmon, flash like the trout," Odhar chanted. He then shoved Matt into the icy water.

CHAPTER 5

With his new height and strength, Matt was surprised at how fast he could move through the water. He figured he would need all the help he could get to rescue his brother. Matt swam through schools of silvery trout and splashed passed salmon larger than cats.

When Matt thought his lungs were about to explode from lack of air, he saw Odhar slip through a huge curtain of sword-shaped sea plants. Matt kicked hard, gliding through the plants and found himself suddenly on solid ground. He took a deep breath of air. "Phew," Matt coughed, "the air in here is foul. Smells like the inside of an old gym bag."

"We are in the Tunnel of the Monster Eels," Odhar explained. "Their teeth are razor sharp, so beware."

"Oh, great," grumbled Matt. Without thinking, he chewed his gum a little harder.

"I think it is time we made ourselves small," Odhar said. He shook the water from his head like a dog.

Matt's eyes widened with surprise. "Hey, wait a minute, if the eels are as bad as you say, we need to be even bigger than we are."

"Take heart, my young friend," said Odhar. "The monster eels have poor eyesight. If we're small, I think we can slip past them."

"Yeah, but if they spot us, we'll be a tasty snack," Matt whispered. He glanced nervously at the huge black holes in the neon green-gold rock walls.

"Small as a bumblebee let us be," Odhar chanted as he squeezed Matt's shoulder harder. Before Matt could argue further, he shrank to the size of a bee.

Matt hurried down the tunnel following Odhar, clutching the pocket knife in his coat pocket. For some odd reason, clutching the steel in his hand bolstered his courage.

They were almost through the tunnel when Matt heard a grinding sound behind him. He spun around. Giant fangs, the size of butcher knives, clanged open and shut inches from him. Above the gnashing teeth, two pulsing green eyes glowed. Matt jumped sideways just as the giant eel lunged forward. Its razor teeth snapped at the air. Matt pressed his back against the rocky wall, praying the poor sighted monster would not see him.

"Odhar, help!" Matt yelled. His voice sounded to his ears no louder than the fluttering of a butterfly's wings. Before Matt could yell again, the monster eel swung its giant head toward him.

Without thinking, Matt jumped. He landed near the eel's eye and grabbed hold of its lower eyelid. With his other hand, Matt plunged his pocket knife into the eel's neon green eye. The eel squirmed and recoiled, throwing Matt to the floor of the tunnel.

"Run for it," Odhar cried.

"Odhar, cast a spell or something," Matt shouted. He could hear the monster eel sliding across the rocks after them.

"I may only do four magic spells a day," answered Odhar, pushing Matt into a tiny hole in the tunnel wall. "We'll hide in here until the eel passes."

Matt's breathing was ragged from running. "Why didn't you tell me you could only do four spells a day?" he gasped.

"Would it have made a difference?" Odhar, grinned.

Odhar and Matt fought the giant eels.

"Do you think the two spells you have left is enough to rescue my brother?" Matt frowned.

They could hear the monster eel gnashing its teeth. It threw its enormous head from side to side as it slithered down the tunnel. After the eel passed their hiding place, both Matt and Odhar sighed with relief.

They jumped back down onto the tunnel floor and ran. Reaching a place where the tunnel forked right and left, they stopped. "Now where?" asked Matt.

"Left," said Odhar. "The Baron's great hall is but a few feet away."

"Let's go," said Matt starting off. He was worried they had wasted precious time hiding from the monster eel.

Once again, Odhar's hand clamped down on Matt's shoulder. "Wait. We can not go into the hall tiny as bees. We will get stuck in one of Baron

35

Everil's webs."

"What are you talking about?" Matt asked, impatiently.

Odhar tightened his hold on Matt. "Tall as we were…"

"Wait," cried Matt. "You're using up another spell. We'll only have one left."

"We have no choice. Small as we are now, we will be captured when we enter the great hall." Odhar continued, "… let us be."

"Here we go again," thought Matt. He felt his body shoot up ten feet, growing thicker and stronger. His head bumped on the rocks of the tunnel ceiling. Matt rubbed his head and hurried after Odhar who was already entering Baron Everil's great hall.

CHAPTER 6

Matt drew back in horror as they entered Baron Everil's great hall. Spider webs, larger than fishing boat nets, crisscrossed the ceiling and walls. Skulls and bones of animals lay trapped and hanging in the glittering webs. "This evil Baron must have a big appetite," Matt whispered.

"We are in luck. Baron Everil is not here. We must free your brother and return to the forest before he returns." Odhar nodded his head toward the back corner of the giant hall. "See those warrior ants? I think they guard your brother."

Matt's mouth dropped open. He had thought the ants were horses. Who would believe ants as big as horses?

He shuddered as he stared at the circle of giant ants. They did seem to be guarding something.

"Wait. We can't go over there bare-handed," Matt cried. He scanned the floor, looking for something to use as a weapon.

Odhar grabbed two bones the size of cow leg bones and threw one to Matt. "Here. Now come on, boy."

Matt gripped the bone with both hands and swung it a few times like he was hitting a baseball. As he crossed the great hall with Odhar, the thought of rescuing his brother chased all fear from his mind.

As Matt and Odhar drew closer to the circle of giant ants, a red ant with fierce, black eyes spotted them. The red ant let out a high-pitched, screeching noise that alerted the others. Four ants broke off from the circle and raced forward to attack.

Matt raised his weapon and started

swinging the leg bone. He heard a cracking sound as he hit one of the ants in the side. It stumbled back and fell over. Another huge beast rushed in. Matt swung again, cracking another ant's shell, then another and another. Out of the corner of his eye, Matt saw Odhar battling another group of ants.

A huge black ant came at Matt from the side. Its front legs wrapped around Matt's ankle and squeezed. "Get off me," screamed Matt, bringing the bone down hard on the black ant's back. It cracked open but still the ant held Matt's ankle. It sank its jaws into Matt's flesh. Matt screamed with pain. He brought his other leg up and smashed his foot down on the ant's head. The ant loosened its grip and Matt kicked it away.

Spinning first right, then left, Matt readied himself for another attack. Fallen ants lay all around him like giant boulders.

"Over here, boy," yelled Odhar.

Matt jerked his head in Odhar's direction. The woodsman was on his back wrestling a giant red ant, its front legs wrapped around Odhar's neck. Matt could also see two other ants moving in.

"Hold on, Odhar," Matt yelled as he charged the two advancing ants. The ants snarled and hissed at Matt. He swung at them over and over until they lay sprawled on the floor. As he stepped toward the ant attacking Odhar to land a killing blow, a hairy antenna whipped around his leg. Matt fell hard, his weapon skittering across the rocky floor.

Matt kicked free of the antenna and threw himself on the back of the ant squeezing Odhar's neck. A sucking sound came from the ant's mouth as it twitched toward Matt's face.

Matt stared into the yawning mouth of the ant. Slime dripped from the insect's jaws. Matt chewed his gum hard, and a rush of saliva filled his mouth. The ant lowered its head to bite.

Matt suddenly remembered every part of him was now bigger. He reared back and shot a bucketful of spit into the ant's face. The ant recoiled, loosening its grip on Odhar.

"Aiyeeeee," Odhar bellowed, throwing the ant and Matt from his body. Once on his feet, Odhar swung his leg bone at the ant, hitting it until it stopped moving.

"Thanks, boy," Odhar exclaimed, helping Matt to his feet. "I thought it was the end for me."

"I don't think the battle is over," Matt answered. He nodded in the direction of the advancing ants. "We need some of your magic now, Odhar."

Odhar shook his head. "I've only one spell left, and we'll be needing that to get you home." He shouldered his weapon and started forward toward the advancing ants. "You have magic in you, boy. After these ants, we will find your brother. Think on that and come on."

The thought of Adam nearby sent a bolt of courage through Matt. He picked up his weapon and charged at the advancing ants.

"You won't stop me," cried Matt. He swung his weapon like a baseball bat striking the ants with thundering blows. Close by, he could hear Odhar's weapon make cracking sounds as it connected with the insects.

Suddenly, the great hall was quiet. Matt looked around and saw giant ants lying everywhere. Matt looked at Odhar and grinned. Then he spun to look at the place the ants had been guarding.

"Oh, no! Odhar, look what the Baron has done to my brother," Matt cried.

CHAPTER 7

Adam was lying in the center of the biggest spider web Matt had ever seen. White rope-like threads were spun around his body, enfolding him in a cocoon. Only his face showed. His eyes were closed.

"What has the evil Baron done to my brother? He looks like a mummy," Matt said.

"He has wrapped your brother in a cocoon. He is saving him to eat later," Odhar explained.

"Is he dead?" Matt asked. His heart beat wildly inside his chest.

"No, he's in a deep sleep," said Odhar. He ran his beefy hand over his face like he was pondering a problem.

"I'm going to get him out of the

cocoon," Matt said. He reached to grab the web, but Odhar stopped him.

"Wait! The web is stickier than an anteater's tongue," Odhar cautioned.

"Well, do something then." Matt said angrily. "Use the last spell. You said you had one left."

"No, we will need it later. We must find something to cut through the sticky ropes." Odhar hurried off to find something sharp, leaving Matt staring at his sleeping brother.

Matt hated seeing his brother lying in the giant web. He jammed his hand into his jeans pocket and pulled out his pocket knife. It had grown larger when Matt turned ten feet tall.

Without asking Odhar, Matt began hacking his way through the slimy white threads of the giant web. Sticky goo dripped onto Matt's hands. Every time he sliced into a new thread, a strange silvery powder blew into his face.

44

The silvery powder gave off an odor. Matt thought of the flowers he had smelled in his mother's garden. The memory drew him in like a hug. His eyes grew heavy, and he stopped hacking at the threads. Suddenly, the sticky goo began to harden on Matt's hands and clothes. The tightening of the sticky goo shocked Matt back to the present.

"Get off me," Matt cried, as he hacked at the sticky goo with his pocket knife.

Fear uncurled inside Matt's mind. "Odhar, help me!" Matt screamed. He was afraid he, too, was becoming stuck in the Baron's web.

"For nature's sake, lad. Did I not tell you to wait until I found something to cut the sticky threads?" Odhar said. He waded into the gooey web up to his waist.

"I thought my pocket knife would cut this stuff," Matt said, slicing and chopping with his knife.

"Your pocket knife is no match for this," said Odhar. "And do not breathe in that powdery white stuff. There is a sleep potion in that powder. Breathe in enough and you will be in dreamland for many a day," Odhar advised.

He tossed Matt a large black glass-like rock called obsidian. "Use this to cut the goo. It won't stick to the rock."

Matt caught the rock, sharp side down. Using the black rock like a long razor, Matt worked his way toward Adam.

Looking at his brother's face, Matt cried, "Don't die on me, Adam. We'll get you out of this evil place." Anger drove the tears from Matt as he lashed out at a huge sticky thread.

Matt could hear Odhar's heavy breathing as he worked next to him. Puffs of powdery poison filled the air each time they cut into a new thread.

Matt coughed and spat, trying not to breathe in the poisonous air. Finally, they reached Adam.

"Leave him be, lad," ordered Odhar. He put his hand on Matt's hand to stop him from cutting the threads of the cocoon.

Matt yanked his hand away from Odhar. His face was bright red with rage. "How can you say such a thing? What if he can't breathe?"

"He can breathe. Trust me. Since he will not be waking, I think he will be easier to carry this way," Odhar explained.

Matt shook his head. "No. I want to cut him free. Besides, I'm ten feet tall, thanks to you. I can easily carry him."

Again, Odhar stopped Matt's hand from slicing another thread. "You can carry him in the cocoon. It is not safe for him to wake up in this place. Remember, I know about these things."

Matt cried, "Don't die on me, Adam! We'll get you out of this evil place."

Matt thought for a moment, a mix of emotions across his face. Finally, he nodded. "Well, let's go."

Odhar and Matt lifted the cocoon on to their shoulders like they were carrying a big log. Carefully, they retraced their steps, backing out of the web the way they had entered.

Their footsteps echoed on the rocky floor as they hurried across the great hall. As they entered the tunnel, Matt heard a deafening flapping sound behind them. He glanced back over his shoulder.

A giant bat with a four foot wing span was hovering near the ceiling. Red laser-like beams shot from the bat's beady eyes.

"Odhar, there's a giant bat following us," Matt shouted.

Odhar picked up the pace. "Whatever you do, do not look directly at the bat's eyes," he instructed.

"Why? Aren't bats blind?" asked

Matt. He hurried to keep up with Odhar so he would not drop his end of the cocoon.

"Not these bats," explained Odhar. "They can make you into a piece of Swiss cheese in less than a minute once they lock their eyes on you."

The bat continued to hover near Matt's head. He could feel the monster bat breathing down his neck. The hairs on the back of Matt's head stood up.

"Walk faster, Odhar. This bat is breathing down my neck," Matt screamed.

"Hang on, lad," Odhar warned, "We are almost to the fork in the tunnel. Do not look back!"

The giant bat swooshed closer. Its huge rubbery wings flapping together made a dreadful sound in the quiet tunnel.

As they neared the fork in the tunnel, the bat swooped past them, its feet raking Matt's head. Matt screamed.

The giant bat hovered in the tunnel exit, blocking their way. Its red laser like eyes swept over them like search lights chasing an escaped prisoner.

CHAPTER 8

"Do not look at the light," yelled Odhar. He turned away from the exit guarded by the huge bat.

Matt rounded the corner following Odhar. He did not want to go down another tunnel passageway, but he had no choice as he was carrying the other end of the cocoon containing his brother.

"I wonder where this tunnel will take us? Up and out, I hope," Matt thought to himself. He felt trapped in an unending maze.

The new tunnel was darker than the tunnel they had been in. Matt could hear water dripping down the sides of the walls. The air was colder and smelled like rotting fish.

"Watch out!" Odhar yelled.

Matt heard Odhar's yell at the same time he felt his feet slip out from under him. He slid on his back down a long wet ramp, like a giant water slide. He tightened his grip on the cocoon with Odhar tumbling along.

Terrified, Matt shouted, "No-o-o-o," as he slid faster and faster. Icy water sprayed his face and soaked his clothes. The cocoon bumped against Matt, hitting him with the force of a boxer's punches to the face and body.

Suddenly, the water slide came to an end. Matt and Odhar tumbled a few feet to the floor. The suddenness of the drop caused them to let go of Adam. The cocoon slid across the floor.

Matt squinted. The cave-like room was painfully bright. Enormous ice crystals hung from the ceiling and grew from the walls. Cold blue light reflected off every surface in the room. In the center of the cave was a huge pile of gold rocks. Sitting on the rocks was a 600-pound man with pale pink eyes and the whitest skin Matt had ever seen.

Matt and Odhar scrambled to their feet. "Is that Baron Everil?" Matt whispered to Odhar.

"Who else would I be?" Baron Everil answered. He laughed like a squealing pig as he rubbed his chubby hands together. "Woodsman Odhar, I wondered if it was you invading my kingdom. You never learn, do you?"

"Evil will never triumph over goodness," Odhar said firmly. He stood tall and unafraid.

Baron Everil laughed scornfully. "Oh, Odhar, that saying is so old. Can't you come up with something more modern?"

"Take the spell off my brother," Matt ordered, feeling suddenly bold. "Or we'll …"

"Or you'll what, boy? Hurt me?"

Baron Everil laughed again. He slapped his chubby hand down on the rock pile making the whole room tremble like an earthquake.

The swaying and rocking of the room made Matt feel sick. He pulled another piece of gum from his pocket and popped it in his mouth.

"Let the boy and his brother go, Baron. There is already a search party coming for them," Odhar said.

"You are very amusing, Odhar. You know as well as I do, no human will ever find this place. Besides, in a few moments, the Winter of Darkness begins. I have not eaten for almost a hundred years, and I am very hungry. I shall just add you both to my menu." Baron Everil grinned and rubbed his hands together like he was staring at two sirloin steaks.

Frightened, Matt glanced sideways at Odhar. He could hear his own heart beating. "Time for the last spell,

Odhar," he whispered.

Baron Everil's pink eyes bulged and his ears twitched. "I think not," he thundered, pointing at Matt. A lightening bolt exploded in front of Matt, barely missing him.

Matt gasped and jumped back. When he glanced again at Baron Everil, he could not believe his eyes. The Baron had changed himself into a giant white spider with legs seven feet long.

"Baron had changed himself into a giant white spider."

"Come on, boy, run for it," Odhar shouted. They headed for the cocoon containing Adam.

Matt grabbed his end of the cocoon and lifted it to his shoulder. "Use your last spell, Odhar. Use it now," Matt cried.

"No, I will need it later," Odhar said stubbornly.

Matt was about to argue with Odhar when Baron Everil shot a strand of goo in their direction. The thread missed as Matt and Odhar jumped out of the way. Again, the Baron shot out a thick rope thread. The second one wrapped around Matt's legs.

"Get off me," Matt cried. He ripped at the sticky cord with his hands.

Baron Everil laughed. "I have you now, boy." Then he sent another thread that whipped around Matt's waist.

"Help, Odhar!" Matt screamed. But Odhar was heading toward the tunnel dragging the cocoon. Matt spun his head and saw Odhar leaving.

"Use your magic now, boy," Odhar commanded.

"My magic?" Matt thought to himself. He was positive that Odhar had lost his mind.

"Do not worry about the woodsman, boy," giggled Baron Everil. His pink spider eyes twinkled with amusement. "He will not get far."

Slowly, like a fisherman with a fish on the line, Baron Everil began reeling in Matt.

Matt worked his jaw, chewing his gum faster. His mind raced. "What magic do I have?" Matt wondered.

The evil Baron Everil chuckled as his front leg shot out and lifted Matt into the air. "Hmmm. A tasty snack," Baron Everil said. His long spidery tongue flicked out and licked Matt's face.

"Ugh," cried Matt with disgust.

"Your breath is nasty, old man."

Baron Everil hissed and his pink eyes glowed red. His spider mouth opened wide, revealing a double set of razor sharp teeth. He thrust his head forward, bringing the teeth inches from Matt's face.

CHAPTER 9

Matt struggled with the sticky cords binding him.   Baron Everil grinned and lowered his spider head closer to Matt's face.

"I usually like to suck the insides out of the body. In your case, I'm just going to bite off your little head." Baron Everil laughed. He played with Matt like a cat playing with a mouse.

Matt's stomach churned with anger. "You're not going to eat me," he thought to himself. But he knew he had to do something quick. Baron Everil would soon tire of torturing him.

Suddenly, an idea struck him. He remembered he was ten feet tall, which meant the gum he was chewing was bigger too. He chomped down on it, giving it a couple of good chews. "May I have one last request before you bite my head off?" Matt asked politely.

"What is the request?" the Baron asked suspiciously.

"Could you change back into a human form? You looked so kingly," said Matt.

Baron Everil thought for a moment. "Kingly, did you say?"

"Very much like a great lord. Master of the Universe," Matt said.

"Oh, well, yes. I do look better in human form," agreed Baron Everil. He shook his spider body, sending a lightning bolt skittering across the floor. He changed back into the human form of a giant six hundred pound man.

Matt held himself very still in Baron Everil's hand. "I'm ready to die now," he said bravely.

Baron Everil's pink eyes glowed, and his tongue licked across his lips.

He slowly lowered his head to bite Matt.

With his free hand, Matt took the big wad of gum out of his mouth and smeared it in Baron Everil's face. The thin layer of gum stuck to the Baron's eyelashes, nose and mouth. Matt flipped out his pocket knife and sank it into the Baron's neck.

Rearing back, Baron Everil howled. He dropped Matt and put his hands to his face and neck. Released from the Baron's grip, Matt fell to the floor.

Without looking back, Matt ran as fast as he could toward the tunnel. As he entered the dark opening, he could still hear the Baron yelling.

"Where's Odhar? I need to get out of here and fast," Matt thought.

He came to a stop at the bottom of the water slide. As his eyes adjusted to the darkness, he noticed a set of stairs built into the wall next to the slide. Taking two steps at a time, he began to climb.

An earthquake tremor rocked the tunnel. Tiny rocks and dirt showered down on Matt as he climbed. In the distance, he could hear Baron Everil raging and stomping his feet. Matt climbed faster.

"I can't believe Odhar left me down here alone," he mumbled. When he reached the top of the water slide, the earth shook like a volcano ready to blow.

Giant bats fluttered in the air, and monster eels slid across the rocks to curl back in their holes. More dirt and rocks fell on Matt as he ran. He didn't stop. He knew without looking back that Baron Everil was coming after him.

Finally, he reached the waterfall. Taking a deep breath, he jumped into the water and kicked out, then upward.

As he surfaced the water, Matt felt himself being lifted from the pool by a strong hand.

"It is about time you got here, lad," Odhar said. "I was starting to worry about you."

Spitting water, Matt stared at Odhar. "Well, you weren't much help. You could have used your last spell."

Odhar grinned. "Why waste a spell when I knew you would do just fine? You mastered your fear and out smarted Baron Everil. Besides, I need the spell for now."

"Now? We're not in any danger now!" Matt cried. He didn't notice that the ground continued to shake.

"If you stay in this time and place, you will never be free of the evil Baron. I know. I have fought him since time began." Odhar reached out and gripped Matt's shoulder. "Back to your size and time, let you be."

When Odhar released his grip on Matt, Matt fell forward into the snow. He landed on his brother Adam who lay asleep next to a half buried log.

"Adam! Oh, my gosh, Adam," cried Matt. He lifted his brother's head from the snow and cradled it in his lap. Adam didn't open his eyes. Frightened, Matt patted his brother's face trying to wake him.

"Odhar, help! My brother isn't waking up. He isn't waking up," Matt shouted. He glanced around and didn't see Odhar anywhere. Matt was alone with his brother Adam.

The forest was quiet. The snow had stopped falling, and stars twinkled in the dark sky.

"What happened?" Adam asked, opening his eyes and looking up at Matt.

Matt grinned with relief. He thought about telling his brother about Odhar, the evil Baron Everil and the waterfall, but Adam was already pushing himself up to a sitting position.

"Somehow we got separated. When I couldn't find you, I went for help, then I came back looking for you," explained Matt. He shrugged his shoulders like it was no big deal.

Adam got to his feet, using Matt's arm to steady himself. "You came back in the dark?" Adam asked.

"Yeah, I sort of overcame my fear," Matt laughed. He wondered to himself what his brother would think if he knew the whole story. Matt looked himself over. He was back to his normal size. He took a step and winced with pain. His sprained ankle was back, too.

In the distance, Matt could hear dogs barking. The search party was on its way.